A Curious
Collection of Cats

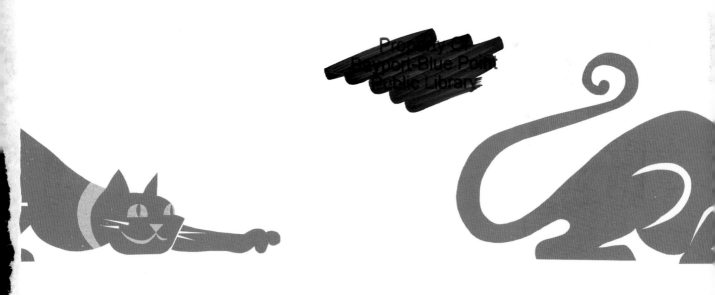

A Curious Collection of Cats

Concrete poems by Betsy Franco

Illustrations by Michael Wertz

Tricycle Press
Berkeley | Toronto

Tricycle Press
an imprint of Ten Speed Press
PO Box 7123
Berkeley, California 94707
www.tricyclepress.com

Typeset in Adrianna Demibold Extended
The illustrations in this book were started in pencil and finished using monoprints and Adobe Photoshop.

Library of Congress Cataloging-in-Publication Data

Franco, Betsy.
  A Curious Collection of Cats / by Betsy Franco ; illustrations by Michael Wertz.
     p. cm.
  ISBN-13: 978-1-58246-248-6
  ISBN-10: 1-58246-248-8
  1. Cats--Juvenile poetry. 2. Children's poetry, American. I. Wertz, Michael, ill. II. Title.
  PS3556.R3325C87 2009
  811'.54--dc22
                            2008011359

First Tricycle Press printing, 2009
Printed in China
1 2 3 4 5 6 — 13 12 11 10 09

ACKNOWLEDGMENTS

For Lincoln, Jada, Frida, Toby, Stoney, Harry and Arturo,
Brownie and Genêt, Angus, Millie and Rosie, Patch,
Samantha, Cocoa and Eliza, the gray kitty, the bad kitty,
the Lincoln-look-alike kitty, Buffy, Dante, Mr. Boo and Miss Binky,
Leo, Louie, The Broiler, August, and Q-tip.

—B.F.

I would like to give deep thanks and appreciation to
my husband, Andy, for his love and attention while I was frantically
drawing cats for this book. Thanks to Miss Olive for getting me out
of the house and for being the best dog in the world.
Thanks to Isabel and Marcos for their talent and encouragement.
Thanks to Abigail for being a great editor.

—M.W.

balancing act

KABOB'S AN AGILE ATHLETE.

HIS BALANCE IS SUBLIME.

EVEN FALLING UPSIDE DOWN,

HE LANDS UPRIGHT EACH TIME.

shadow's dream

MOONLIGHT GHOSTLY AND PURE, POURED THROUGH THE WINDOW, ROUSING SHADOW

FROM HER

COUCH-SCRATCH-ING

MOUSE-

CATCH-ING

DREAMS

SHE STARES AT NOTHING WHEN IT FLUTTERS AND TWITCHES, POUNCES AND GRABS IT WHENEVER IT ITCHES. THOUGH IT CERTAINLY COULDN'T EXIST ALL ALONE, TABITHA'S TAIL HAS A LIFE OF ITS OWN.

a question for scooter about squirrels

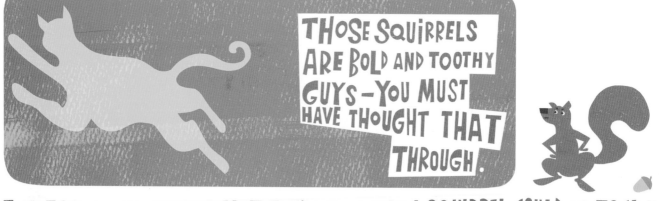

I GUESS YOU'D RATHER NOT FIND OUT WHAT A SQUIRREL COULD DO TO YOU.

a tomcat's yard is his kingdom

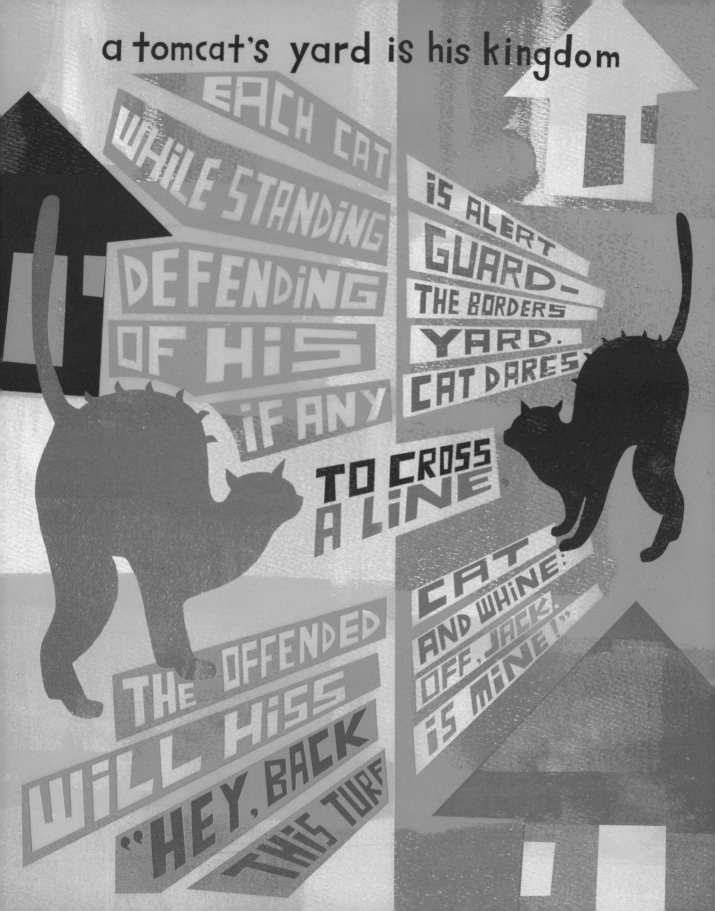

EACH CAT
WHILE STANDING
DEFENDING
OF HIS
IF ANY

IS ALERT
GUARD-
THE BORDERS
YARD.
CAT DARES

TO CROSS
A LINE.

CAT
AND WHINE:
OFF, JACK.
IS MINE!"

THE OFFENDED
WILL HISS
"HEY, BACK
THIS TURF

Veronica Goes Wide

VERONICA USED TO BE TINY AND FAST, BUT SINCE SHE WAS SMALL, MANY BIRTHDAYS HAVE PASSED. VERONICA'S GOTTEN SO PUDGY, AND PLUMP, SHE NOW MOSTLY ACTS LIKE A SNUGGABLE LUMP.

FROM DANGLING Q-TIP IS THE Q-TIP IS

ROSIE'S MOUTH, THERE'S NO REAL CAUSE FOR ALARM. FOR ROSIE ADORES HER PORTABLE PAL. SHE DOESN'T INTEND ANY HARM. WHEN Q-TIP IS BORED WITH ROSIE'S GAME OF CARTING HIM TO AND FRO, HE SOFTLY SWATS HER ON THE NOSE, AND ROSIE LETS HIM GO!

gonzo's snack

JUMPING FOR A MOURNING DOVE AND SETTLING FOR A

THE DEEP · RHYTHMIC · RRRRRETCH

OF THE TABBY'S GAGS AND COUGHS ·

NASTY HAIRBALL

A TREE FOR SAMANTHA

SOME CATS CAN SENSE THE WAY YOU FEEL — MY SAM WAS ONE OF THOSE.

SHE KNEW MY SAD, MY ANGRY, MY BUMMED, MY HAPPY-DOWN-TO-MY-TOES.

THE OLDER SHE GOT, THE SLOWER SHE GOT, — HER LIFE CAME TO A CLOSE.

TO HONOR HER, WE BOUGHT AN OAK. IT'S PLANTED BY THE ROSE.

THE OAK IS STRONG, AND IT WILL MAKE GOOD CLIMBING WHEN IT GROWS.

BUT IT WILL NEVER GUESS I'M SAD AND KISS ME ON THE NOSE.

RASCAL'S TONGUE

IF YOU'VE EVER ATTEMPTED TO LICK YOUR NECK CLEAN, I THINK YOU'LL UNDERSTAND WHAT I MEAN. GO AHEAD, LICK YOUR NECK. WHEN I SAY MY CAT'S TONGUE IS ESPECIALLY LONG, PROVE ME WRONG!

YOGA CAT POSE

that cat peed on my hat
THE WEEK THAT WE WENT OUT OF TOWN, DELILAH WAS FEELING DOWN.
SHE WASN'T JUST LONELY AND SAD. THAT CAT WAS STEAMING MAD.
SHE DISCOVERED MY BRAND-NEW HAT
AND PEED ALL OVER THAT.
IN GETTING HER MESSAGE ACROSS,
SHE SHOWED ME WHO'S THE BOSS!

BINGO'S BIRTHDAY PARTY

We scattered toy mice all over the floor and hung purple yarn from every door.

The guest list was short — just Calico Kate, 'cause she's the one cat that he'll tolerate.

The special dessert was tricky to make, a sardine and shrimp-flavored birthday cake.

EAR DECORATIONS

kissy kat

TECHNO CAT
SEND TO: TECHNO_CAT@CATMAIL.COM
FROM: ME@CATMAIL.COM
WHEN WRITING FRIENDS AN EMAIL
I SOMETIMES &p*&%^$#
HAVE A FIT
IF MITCHELL WALKS ACROSS THE KEYS
k:j^$% AND ADDS A NOTE
vpq#peifgu3gy TO IT!

MISS BOO, WHOSE OPINIONS WERE STRONG, THOUGHT THAT LEASHING A CAT WAS ALL WRONG. SHE PULLED AND SHE CRIED, SHE WAS FIT TO BE TIED, THOUGH HER LEASH WAS 100 FEET LONG!